SHARON E. McKAY · DANIEL LAFRANCE

WAR BROTHERS
The Graphic Novel

Art by Daniel Lafrance

annick press
toronto + new york + vancouver

Adapted from *War Brothers*, copyright © 2008 Sharon E. McKay, published by Puffin Canada

Annick Press Ltd.

We acknowledge the support of the Canada Council for the Arts, the Ontario Arts Council,
and the Government of Canada through the Canada Book Fund (CBF) for our publishing activities.

ONTARIO ARTS COUNCIL
CONSEIL DES ARTS DE L'ONTARIO

Cataloging in Publication

McKay, Sharon E.
War brothers : the graphic novel / Sharon E. McKay, Daniel Lafrance;
art by Daniel Lafrance.

Adaptation of: War brothers / Sharon McKay.
Issued also in electronic format.
ISBN 978-1-55451-489-2 (bound).—ISBN 978-1-55451-488-5 (pbk.)

1. Child soldiers—Uganda—Comic books, strips, etc. 2. Child soldiers—Uganda—Juvenile fiction.
3. Kidnapping victims—Uganda—Comic books, strips, etc.
4. Kidnapping victims—Uganda—Juvenile fiction. 5. Friendship—Comic books, strips, etc.
6. Friendship—Juvenile fiction. 7. Courage—Comic books, strips, etc.
8. Courage—Juvenile fiction. 9. Graphic novels.
I. Lafrance, Daniel   II. McKay, Sharon E.   War brothers.   III. Title.

PN6733.M45W27 2013   j741.5'971   C2012-906340-1

Distributed in Canada by:
Firefly Books Ltd.
66 Leek Crescent
Richmond Hill, ON
L4B 1H1

Published in the U.S.A. by:
Annick Press (U.S.) Ltd.
Distributed in the U.S.A. by:
Firefly Books (U.S.) Inc.
P.O. Box 1338, Ellicott Station
Buffalo, NY 14205

Printed in China

Visit us at: www.annickpress.com
Visit Sharon E. McKay at: www.sharonmckay.com
Visit Daniel Lafrance at: www.danlafrance.com

To the MacLeod men in my life:
David, Sam, Joe, Richard, Bryan,
Stirling, Kai, and Angus (Gus).

SHARON E. McKAY

To my son Max and my wife Nadia.

DANIEL LAFRANCE

IN EACH OF US THERE IS

THE POSSIBILITY TO BE A BEAST,

BUT ALSO THE POSSIBILITY

TO REACH THE STARS.

—ELEANOR ROOSEVELT

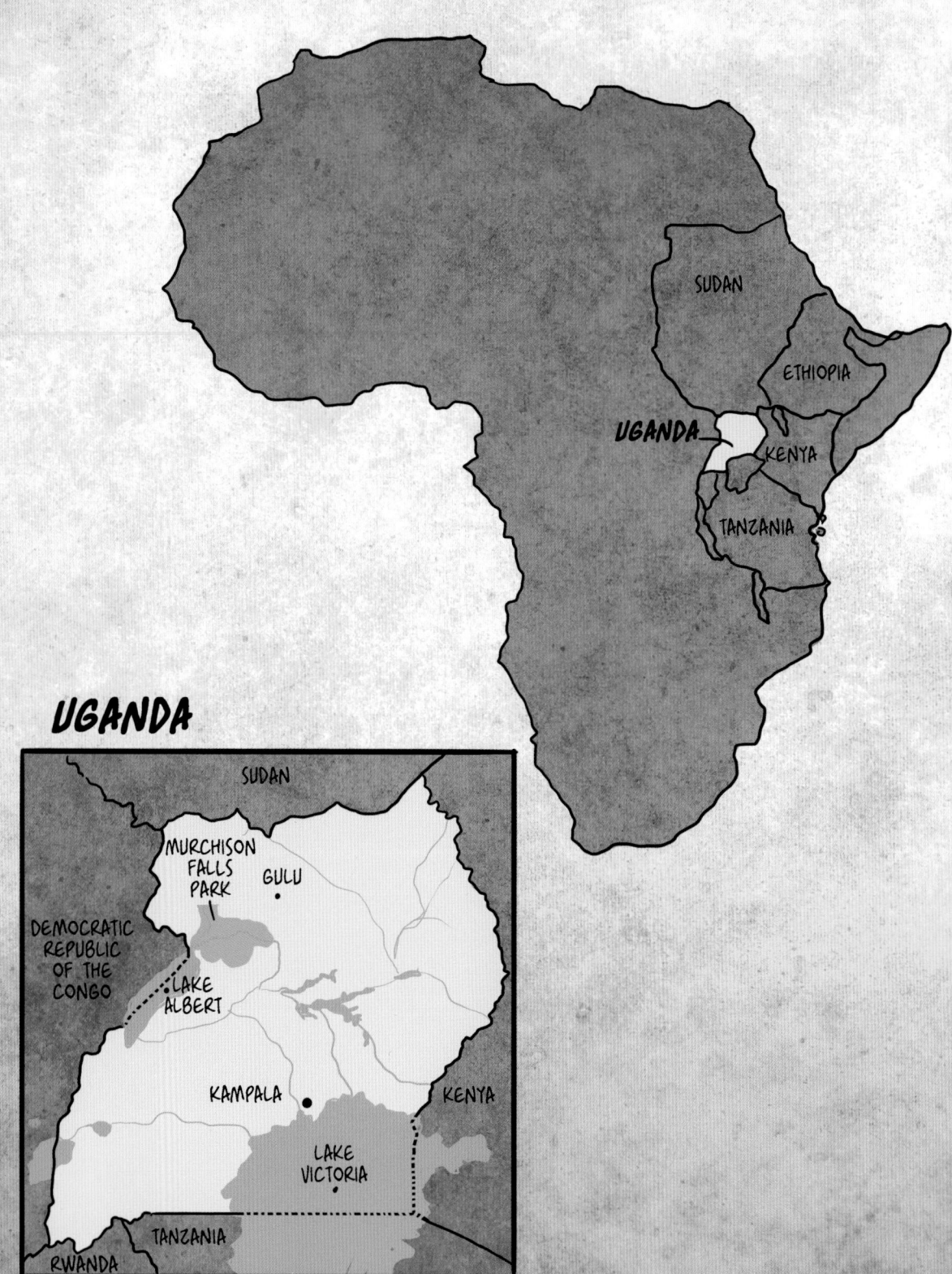

UGANDA

Gulu, Uganda, 2002

Dear Reader

My name is Kitino Jacob. I was born in Gulu, a city of 110,000 people in the north of Uganda. I am from the Acholi tribe.

Where I live, far from the capital city of Kampala, Kony Joseph leads the Lord's Resistance Army (or the LRA) My country knows this man simply as Kony, the leader of an army of abducted children. He and his LRA gang of rebels steal boys and girls from rural farms, villages, schools, and buses. They say that only they know the true christian way, that their army of Christian soldiers will fight the government of Uganda and create a country of Christians called "Acholiland." But Kony and his Lord's Resistance Army are cruel beyond measure. They are not Christians. They do not care for or protect children. I know this to be true because I was one of those abducted children. I became a child soldier in Kony's Army.

My story is not an easy one to tell, and it is not an easy one to read. The life of a child soldier is full of unthinkable violence and brutal death. But this is also a story of hope, courage, friendship, and family. We Ugandans believe that family is most important.

I thought you should be prepared for both the bad and the good. There is no shame in closing this book now.

Jacob

NORTH UGANDA, 2002

THERE IS A CONVOY OF SOLDIERS COMING.

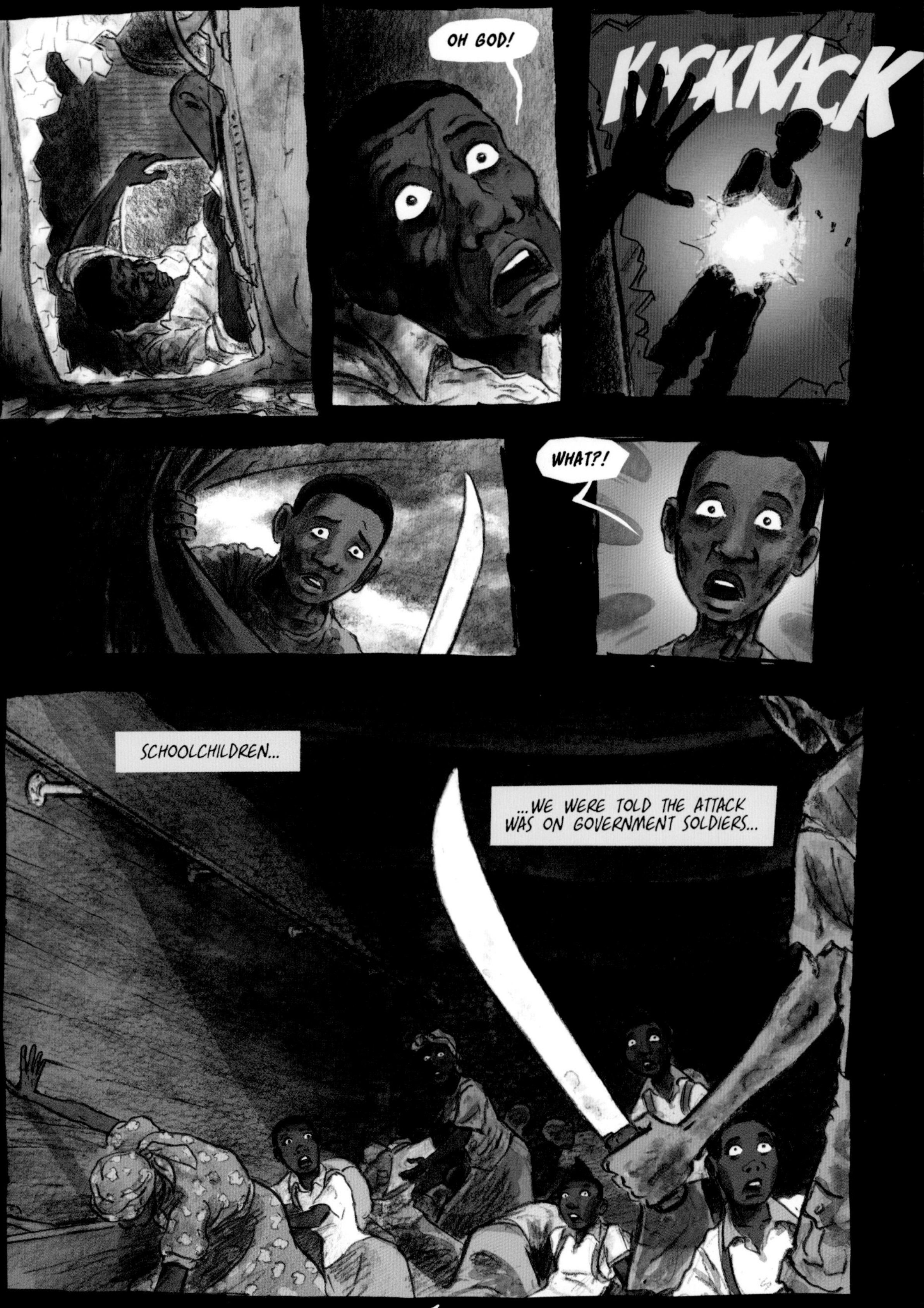

8

KILL THE
MOTHER!!

AND THEN THE WORLD STOOD STILL...
A VOICE...A VOICE IN MY HEAD...
Pussycat, Pussycat, where have you been?

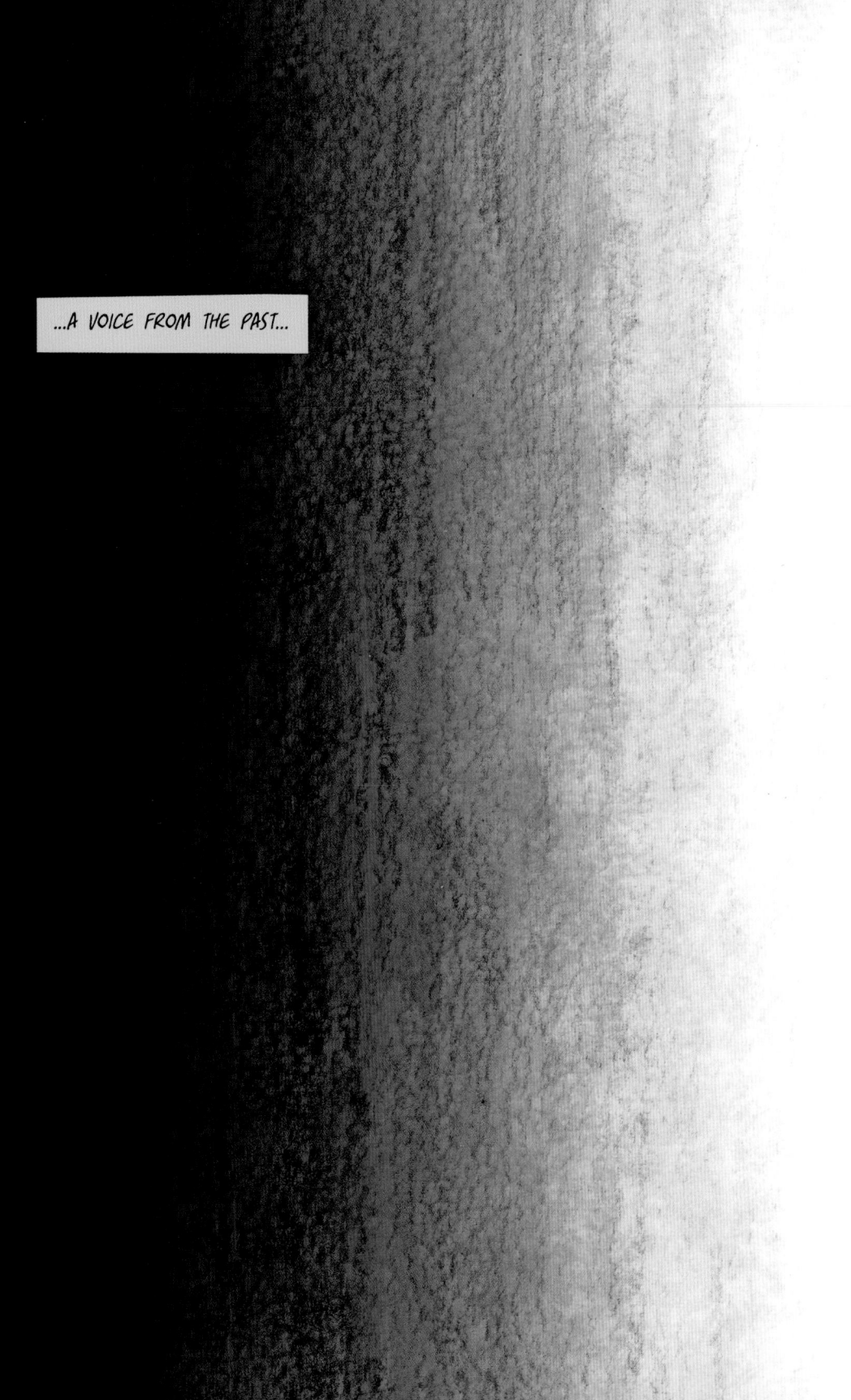

...A VOICE FROM THE PAST...

GULU, TWO MONTHS EARLIER

THUNK!

SCORES!!

THE CROWD GOES WILD!!

JACOB!

WELL THEN, YOU WILL BE THINKING OF YOUR FUTURE, OF UNIVERSITY PERHAPS. WHAT *SUBJECTS* DO YOU LIKE?

HE LIKES MATHEMATICS! JACOB IS THE BEST AT MULTIPLYING IN OUR *WHOLE SCHOOL!*

HE CAN MULTIPLY *ANYTHING!*

STOP IT!

MATHEMATICS, IS IT?

THIS IS MY FRIEND TONY. WE GO TO THE SAME SCHOOL.

GOOD DAY TO YOU, TONY. AND WHERE DO YOU FINE BOYS ATTEND SCHOOL?

PLEASED TO MEET YOU, SIR.

WE GO TO *GEORGE JONES SEMINARY FOR BOYS.* WE LEAVE TOMORROW.

COME, OLD FRIEND! EVERYONE HAS ARRIVED. WE WAIT ONLY FOR YOU.

I HAVE HEARD GOOD THINGS ABOUT THAT SCHOOL...

...GOOD LUCK TO YOU BOTH.

HE SEEMS SAD.

HE IS SAD BECAUSE HIS GRANDSON WAS TAKEN BY **KONY**.

WHAT!!!?

THEY TOOK HIM AS HE WAS WALKING HOME FROM SCHOOL, AND THAT IS THE LAST ANYONE HAS HEARD ABOUT HIM. HE WAS JUST A LITTLE YOUNGER THAN US THEN.

HE WAS SUPPOSED TO BE VERY GOOD IN MATHEMATICS TOO. FATHER TOLD ME.

DID YOU KNOW HIM? MUSA HENRY TORAC'S GRANDSON I MEAN?

NO. HE LIVED IN KITGUM.

KONY IS A **MADMAN**, EVERYONE SAYS SO. HOW ELSE TO EXPLAIN WHY HE ABDUCTS CHILDREN FOR HIS ARMY?

KONY CANNOT GET US. DO **NOT** BE WORRIED. WE ARE **SAFE**. I HEARD FATHER TALKING TO HEADMASTER HAYCOOP ABOUT HIRING **EXTRA GUARDS** TO SURROUND THE SCHOOL.

THERE IS NO REASON TO FEAR KONY AND HIS REBEL SOLDIERS.

THAT'S GOOD.

FATHER MUST TAKE THE CAR TO KAMPALA. I WILL GO TO SCHOOL BY BUS TOMORROW. WE WILL GO TOGETHER.

I WILL MEET YOU AT THE BUS TOMORROW!

BYE, TONY!

IT IS TIME, JACOB.

GO AND STAND IN THE INSIDE COURTYARD WHERE YOUR FATHER CAN SEE YOU. HE WILL CALL YOU WHEN HE IS READY TO TALK.

WHAT DOES **PRESIDENT MUSEVENI** DO ABOUT **KONY** AND HIS ARMY OF CHILDREN UP HERE IN THE NORTH? HE SHOULD SEND US MORE GOVERNMENT SOLDIERS. **OUR PEOPLE** NEED MORE **PROTECTION.**

I WILL TELL YOU, **MUSEVENI** DOES NOT WANT KONY CAUGHT BECAUSE IT GIVES HIM THE EXCUSE TO KEEP SUCH A **BIG ARMY.** BUT THERE IS GREAT CORRUPTION IN THE ARMY.

WHY ARE THEY ALWAYS TALKING POLITICS?

NO, NO, MUSEVENI MAY HAVE TAKEN OVER THE PRESIDENCY BY FORCE, BUT HE HAS SO FAR PROVEN HIMSELF TO BE A **GOOD RULER.**

THINK OF THE 1970S AND GENERAL **IDI AMIN DADA'S** MILITARY RULE.

THIRTY THOUSAND MURDERED. MY OWN BROTHER **KILLED!**

THIS KONY IS OF THE ACHOLI TRIBE, JUST LIKE US, BUT HE ATTACKS MOSTLY US. HE MUST BE **CAUGHT.**

HOW COULD SUCH AN EVIL MAN CONTINUE TO EXIST?

THEY CALL KONY'S SOLDIERS BEASTS, BUT MY GRANDSON IS A GOOD BOY.

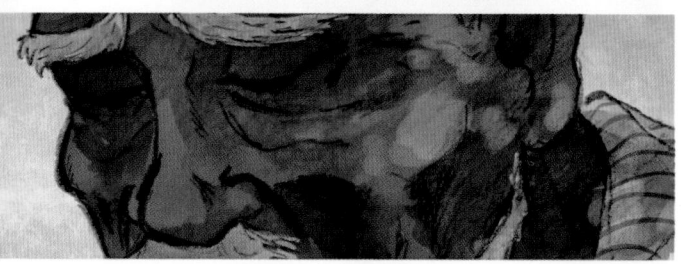

MY GRANDSON'S NAME IS MICHAEL, AFTER *SAINT MICHAEL, THE WARRIOR.* DID NOT SAINT MICHAEL FIGHT SATAN IN HEAVEN? PERHAPS A CHILD WITH SUCH A NAME COULD FIGHT SATAN ON EARTH? AND IS THIS KONY NOT SATAN HIMSELF?

PLEASE EXCUSE ME FOR A MOMENT.

JACOB, MY SON.

FATHER

18

I LEAVE TONIGHT FOR ENGLAND. I WILL NOT SEE YOU AGAIN UNTIL THE NEXT SCHOOL BREAK.

DO YOU REMEMBER THE LAST POEM BOOK I BROUGHT BACK?

"PUSSYCAT, PUSSYCAT, WHERE HAVE YOU BEEN? I'VE BEEN TO LONDON TO VISIT THE QUEEN. PUSSYCAT, PUSSYCAT, WHAT DID YOU DO THERE? I FRIGHTENED A LITTLE MOUSE UNDER HER CHAIR."

YOUR MOTHER *LOVED* READING THAT BOOK TO YOU.

I MISS HER, FATHER.

DO NOT BE SAD. SHE IS WITH GOD, MY SON.

YOUR MOTHER WOULD WANT YOU TO BE HAPPY.

IS THERE ANYTHING I CAN BRING YOU BACK FROM LONDON?

YES, A *FOOTBALL*, SO THAT TONY AND I CAN HAVE *REAL MATCHES!*

HAHA, A FOOTBALL IT IS THEN!

THANK YOU, FATHER!

MAKE ME PROUD THIS SEMESTER DO NOT FORGET THAT YOU ARE *ACHOLI*, A GREAT AND HONORABLE TRIBE.

I WILL, FATHER

NEXT MORNING

VWRRR

VWRRRR

20

THIS ONE?

YES, PLEASE AND THANK YOU!

ARE THESE THE EXTRA GUARDS YOUR FATHER HAD ASKED FOR?

SEE, I TOLD YOU NOT TO WORRY.

GEORGE JONES SEMINARY FOR BOYS

I GET THE MIDDLE.

WE ARE *SAMOSAS!*

YOU ARE THE *STUFFING*, HAHA!

AH, THERE YOU ARE. I HAVE BEEN WAITING TO TALK TO YOU THREE.

SAY HELLO TO OKELLO NORMAN. HE'S NEW HERE AND HE'S YOUNGER THAN THE REST OF YOU, ONLY TWELVE, BUT HE HAS EXCELLED IN ALL HIS CLASSES.

HE IS HERE ON A FULL MATHEMATICS SCHOLARSHIP.

GIVEN YOUR INTEREST IN MATHEMATICS, JACOB, I THOUGHT YOU MIGHT MAKE HIM FEEL WELCOME.

I WANT ALL THREE OF YOU TO BE *RESPONSIBLE* FOR HIM. SEE THAT HIS FIRST FEW WEEKS GO *SMOOTHLY*.

NORMAN, YOU'LL FIT RIGHT IN.
WHY DON'T YOU COME WITH US TO CHURCH TONIGHT?
TOMORROW YOU CAN COME TO CLASS WITH US.

GEORGE JONES SEMINARY
FOR BOYS EXISTS TO PRODUCE SCHOLARS
WHO WILL TAKE OUR GREAT COUNTRY
OF UGANDA INTO THE FUTURE...

...WE MUST THEREFORE AVAIL
OURSELVES OF THE WORLD'S
KNOWLEDGE, BOTH PAST
AND PRESENT.

26

SO THE TWO BULLS CHARGED AT EACH OTHER AND...

...THE HEAD BOY YELLED SO LOUD HE FELL *OUT OF THE TREE!*

HAHAHA!

PAUL, WHAT ABOUT THE TRIP YOU TOOK WITH YOUR FATHER?

YES, TELL US ABOUT *AMERICA!*

WELL, IN NEW YORK CITY THERE'S A TEAM CALLED THE YANKEES. THEY PLAY A GAME LIKE CRICKET BUT NOT AT ALL LIKE CRICKET.

THEY PLAY AT NIGHT, BUT IT LOOKS LIKE DAY.

AND THERE ARE MOVING STAIRCASES, AND THEY EAT DOGS IN BUNS!

AND JACOB, YOUR FATHER HAS MANY BULLS ON HIS FARM, BUT I DRANK RED BULL IN A *CAN!*

LIGHTS OUT, GENTLEMEN!

CLICK!

CLICK!

WHY ARE WE LOCKED IN?

YOU'RE NEW HERE. IT'S TO STOP US FROM RUNNING OFF TO THE GIRLS' SCHOOL DOWN THE ROAD. HAHAHA!

HAHAHA, NO ONE HAS ACTUALLY DONE IT!

PAUL...

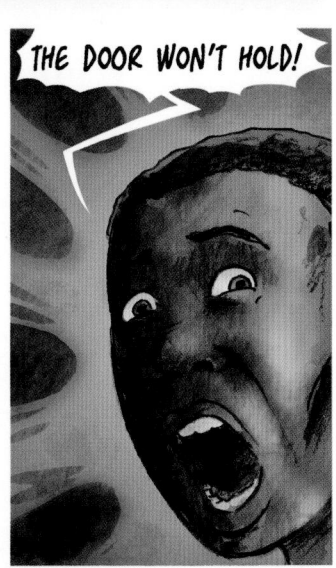

ATTENTION!

CLICK

MY NAME IS COMMANDER OPIRO!

IF ANYONE **CRIES** OR **SCREAMS**, HE WILL BE PUNISHED BY **DEATH**!

YOU WILL BE **SOLDIERS** NOW! YOU WILL FIGHT FOR YOUR **COUNTRY**...

...AND KILL FOR **GOD**!

WAKE UP...

JACOB, YOU
MUST WAKE UP!

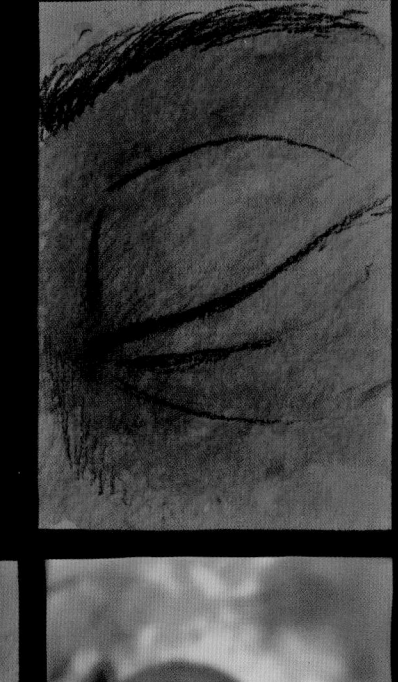

PLEASE, JACOB...

...OPEN YOUR EYES!

MY HEAD...

YOU GOT HIT.
DON'T MAKE ANY SOUND.

WHERE ARE WE?

WE DON'T KNOW. IN THE BUSH.
THEY WERE GOING TO *KILL YOU*. THAT SOLDIER,
THE ONE WITH THE SCARRED FACE, HE'S MEAN.
THEY CALL HIM *LIZARD*.

THE COMMANDER ASKED WHO YOU WERE. I TOLD HIM YOUR NAME. THAT SOLDIER LIZARD MADE US CARRY YOU ALL NIGHT.

LIZARD—HE'S GOT IT OUT FOR YOU, JACOB. NOW THAT YOU ARE AWAKE, YOU HAVE TO WALK ON YOUR OWN, YOU HAVE TO.

WHY ARE YOU TALKING ABOUT A LIZARD?

WHERE ARE OUR TEACHERS?

MR. OJOK WAS LYING ON THE GROUND. MAYBE HE WAS DEAD. WE DID NOT SEE ANY OTHER TEACHERS.

BUT WHAT ABOUT THE EXTRA GUARDS MY FATHER HIRED?

THEY RAN AWAY.

GET UP! TIME TO MARCH!

C'MON, JACOB.

AARGH!

HE WALKS ON HIS OWN OR HE DIES!

HOW LONG HAVE WE BEEN WALKING... TWO DAYS?

I NEED TO REST, BUT TO REST IS TO DIE!

WHERE IS MY FATHER?

WHERE IS THE ARMY WITH ITS MODERN WEAPONS?

WE CAN'T BE THAT HARD TO FIND!

VVRRRR

IT'S COMMANDER OPIRO AGAIN, JACOB. I'M SCARED!

LINE UP STRAIGHT LIKE SOLDIERS!

YOU ARE **REBELS** NOW. YOU FIGHT FOR **FREEDOM**. YOU FIGHT FOR THE **LORD'S RESISTANCE ARMY** AND FOR **GOD**!

KONY IS OUR **LEADER** AND WE DO AS HE **SAYS**!

I SHALL TELL YOU THE **RULES** AND YOU WILL **LISTEN**!

ONLY **SOLDIERS** EAT. IF YOU WANT TO **EAT**, YOU WILL **FIGHT** WITH US. THIS IS **YOUR CHOICE**. IF YOU **DIE** OF HUNGER, IT IS YOUR CHOICE. IF YOU **STEAL FOOD**, YOU WILL BE **KILLED**.

YOU MUST NOT TOUCH **ALCOHOL** OR ANY **DRUGS**. WE ARE ALL CHRISTIANS AND WE MUST OBEY THE **TEN COMMANDMENTS**.

NOW I ASK YOU, DO YOU LIKE **WOMEN**?

WHAT'S THE RIGHT ANSWER? YES? NO? WHAT IF NO MEANS DEATH?

YOU SEE THESE WOMEN? THEY ARE WIVES OF **SOLDIERS**. IF ANY OF YOU ARE CAUGHT **TALKING** TO ANY OF THEM...

...THE WOMAN WILL BE **KILLED** AND YOU WILL BE **BEATEN**!

NOW, I WILL TELL YOU A MOST IMPORTANT RULE...

SNAP!

I WILL SHOW YOU WHAT HAPPENS TO ANYONE WHO TRIES TO *ESCAPE!*

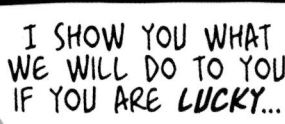

I SHOW YOU WHAT WE WILL DO TO YOU IF YOU ARE *LUCKY...*

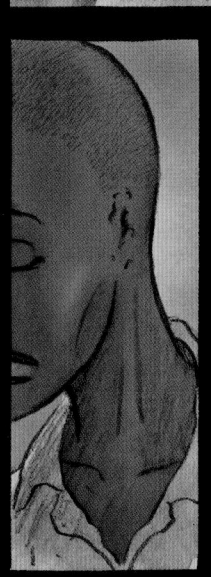

THEY'VE CUT OFF HER EARS!

THIS GIRL MIGHT HAVE BEEN GIVEN TO A COMMANDER, MAYBE TO *KONY HIMSELF.*

BUT LOOK AT HER NOW, SHE IS *WORTHLESS!*

NO MAN WOULD TOUCH HER. IF YOU TRY TO RUN AWAY, I WILL DO THE SAME TO YOU, OR WORSE!

KILL OR BE KILLED.

OH NO... THEY ARE GOING TO BEAT ADAM!

I AM A CATHOLIC. GOD SAID THOU SHALT NOT KILL.

WHAT ARE YOU DOING?

LET ME GO!

OH NO!

PLEASE NO!!

48

WOULD YOU PREFER A **LONG-SLEEVED** OR **SHORT-SLEEVED SHIRT?**

IF YOU WOULD LIKE A LONG-SLEEVED SHIRT, I WILL **TAKE OFF YOUR HAND...**

...BUT IF YOU WOULD LIKE A SHORT-SLEEVED SHIRT, I WILL **TAKE OFF YOUR ARM!**

OUR FATHER, WHO ART IN HEAVEN, HALLOWED BE THY...

YOUR FRIEND WILL **DIE** NO MATTER WHAT YOU DO. HE IS **INJURED.** HE IS OF NO USE.

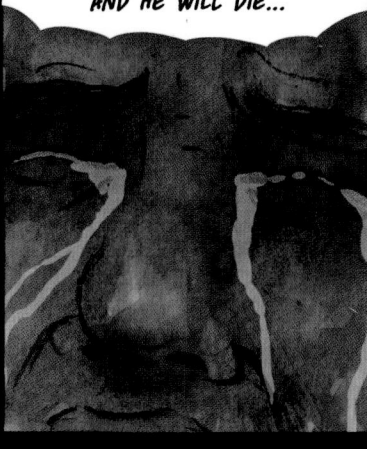

YOU WILL LOSE YOUR ARM AND HE WILL DIE, OR YOU WILL NOT LOSE YOUR ARM AND HE WILL DIE...

...WHAT WILL IT BE?

DO NOT TAKE MY ARM...

YOU START!

NOT TONY. TONY WHO WANTS TO BE A PRIEST.

DEAR GOD, HELP US IN OUR HOUR OF NEED...

WHY DO YOU CLOSE YOUR EYES?

YOU WATCH OR YOU DIE!

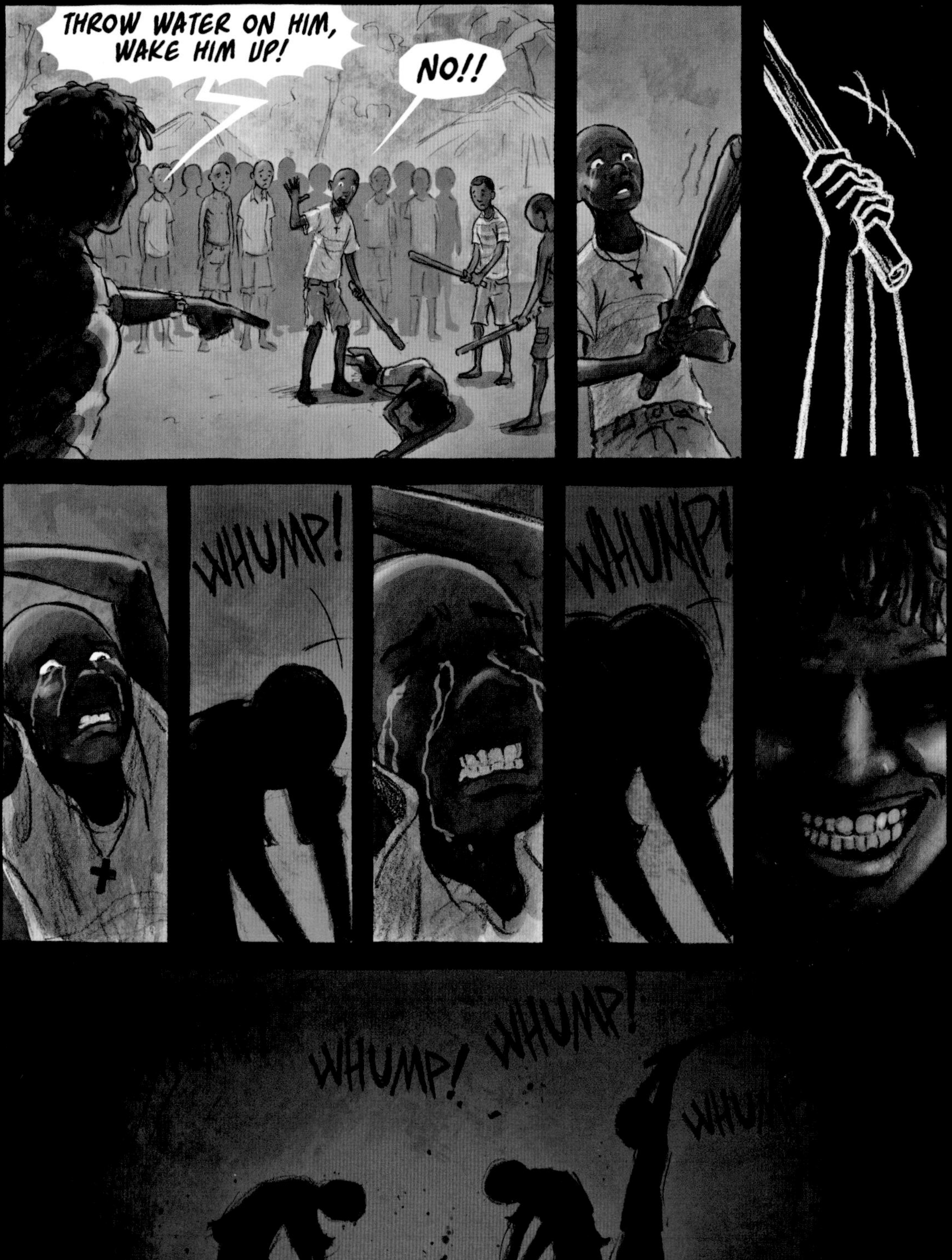

51

ADAM IS DEAD...

WHY DID THIS BOY HAVE TO BE **KILLED**?

HE WAS KILLED BECAUSE HE WAS WEAK. **GOD** ONLY WANTS **STRONG SOLDIERS** TO FIGHT FOR HIM. WE WILL FORCE YOU TO DO **YOUR DUTY** AND FIGHT FOR GOD AND OUR COUNTRY, **ACHOLILAND!**

THESE CHILDREN ARE BORN OF LRA COMMANDERS. THEY ARE **PURE.** THEY WILL ONE DAY RULE **ACHOLILAND.**

THE **UGANDA ARMY** THINKS THEY ARE STRONG. THEY HAVE **HELICOPTERS, TANKS,** AND POWERFUL **MISSILES** BUT THEY HAVE **NO VICTORY.**

WHY? BECAUSE **GOD** IS ON **OUR SIDE.**

DO NOT **FEAR** THE BULLETS FROM A GOVERNMENT GUN. THEIR GUNS ARE USELESS AND THE BULLETS WILL **BOUNCE** OFF YOU LIKE HARD RAIN. A **JESUS CROSS** DRAWN ON YOUR BODY WITH OIL ALSO PREVENTS BULLETS FROM HURTING YOU. LET US **PRAY!**

ON YOUR KNEES!

YOU MUST **FACE THE EAST** TO PRAY TO **GOD** BECAUSE THAT IS WHERE **GOD LIVES.** HANDS TOGETHER AND LOWER YOUR HEADS.

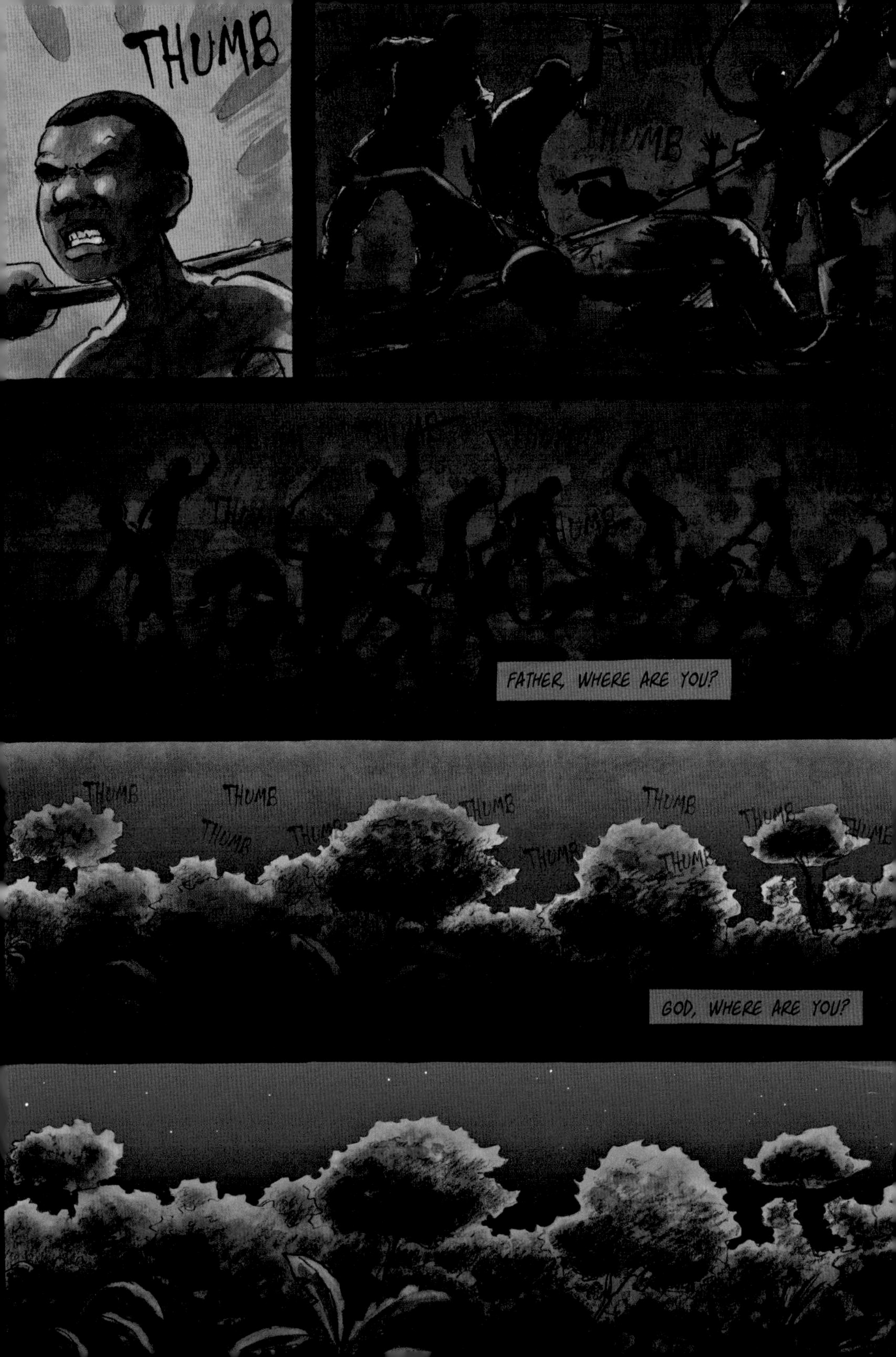

THUMB

FATHER, WHERE ARE YOU?

THUMB THUMB THUMB THUMB THUMB
THUMB THUMB THUMB THUMB
THUMB

GOD, WHERE ARE YOU?

HMMM...

PAUL?

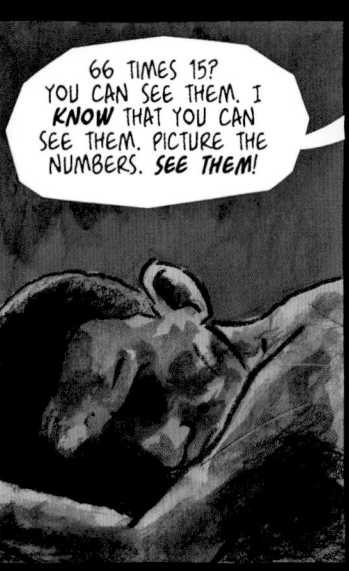

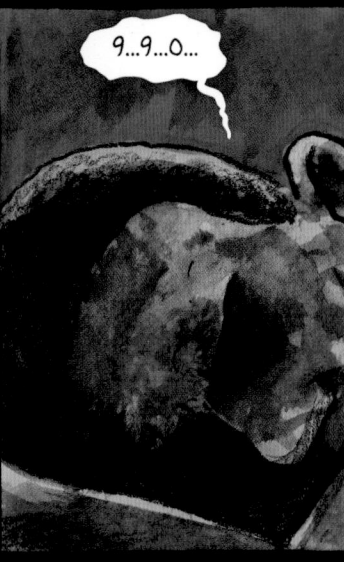

LISTEN TO ME. THE ARMY, OUR **FATHERS**, THEY **WILL** COME. WE HAVE TO STAY TOGETHER. WE HAVE TO TRY TO KEEP EACH OTHER SAFE. WE ARE **BROTHERS**, WE ARE **FAMILY**.

SWEAR TO GOD, THE REAL GOD, SWEAR TO **EACH OTHER**, SWEAR THAT WE ARE **BROTHERS**.

I SWEAR

ME TOO.

TONY, YOU TOO!

WHUMP! WHUMP! WHUMP!

TONY IS DIFFERENT...

...KILLING ADAM HAS **CHANGED** HIM.

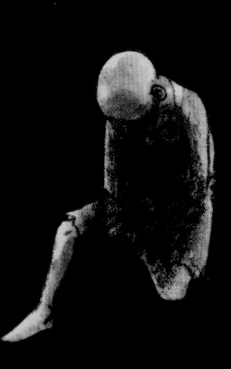

WE WALKED.

THEY TOLD US WE WERE WALKING FOR GOD.

THAT THIS WAS GOD'S WILL.

MOSQUITOES FEASTED ON OUR OPEN WOUNDS.
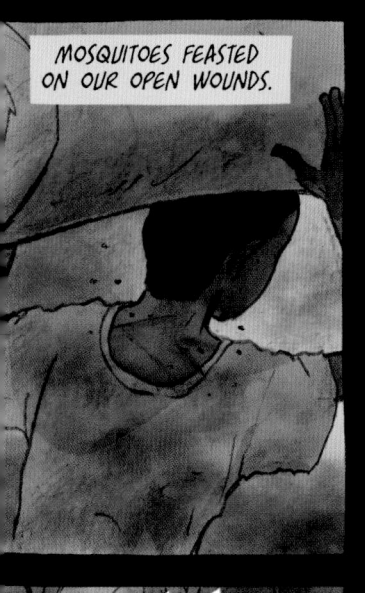

WATER WAS SCARCE.

NUMB LEGS, INFECTED FEET.
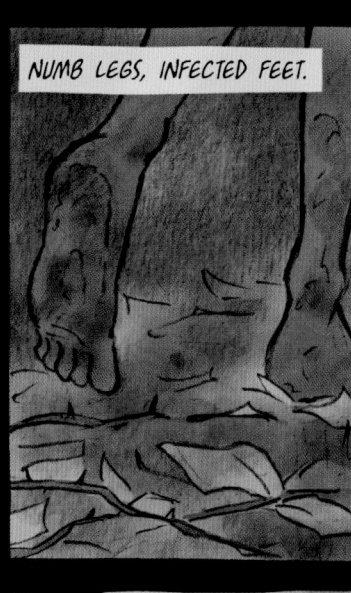

SIT AND BE QUIET!

FOR THE PAIN. PASS IT AROUND. DON'T LET THEM SEE YOU CHEW.

WALK!

WHY DID THAT REBEL SOLDIER HELP US?

THERE WAS A ROUTINE TO OUR DAYS.

NOT ONCE HAD WE WOKEN UP IN THE MORNING AND GONE TO SLEEP AT NIGHT IN THE SAME PLACE.

SCOUTS LED THE WAY THROUGH THE BUSH. THEY WERE SMALL BOYS WHO WERE WELL FED AND RAN FAST. SOME WERE PACES AHEAD, SOME HOURS AHEAD.

EVERYONE HAD A DESIGNATED JOB.

NORMAN, PAUL, AND I WERE SLAVES, LIKE MOST OF THE SCHOOLBOYS.

ONLY SOLDIERS WERE ALLOWED TO DRINK THE WATER AND EAT FOOD. WE ATE WHAT WE COULD SCAVENGE ALONG THE WAY: INSECTS, WILD FRUITS, AND LIZARDS.

TONY AND THE OTHER BOYS WHO HAD KILLED ADAM GOT TRAINING AND GUNS...

...THEY WERE SOLDIERS NOW.

WHEN A SCOUT RETURNED WITH THE NEWS THAT THERE WAS A VILLAGE AHEAD, AN ASSAULT TEAM WAS FORMED AND PREPARED FOR BATTLE. THEY PRAYED, DOUSED THEIR HEADS WITH WATER TO WASH AWAY THEIR SINS, AND TIED MAGICAL STONES AROUND THEIR WRISTS. THEY WENT OFF TO BATTLE WHILE WE WAITED.

WHEN WE WERE TOO EXHAUSTED TO MOVE, THEY WOULD TEACH US ABOUT ARMS, ANTITANK MINES, ANTIPERSONNEL MINES. THE GUNS HAD ENGLISH ALPHABET LETTERS: SPGS, SMGS, BIOS. AND THERE WERE SAM7 MISSILES AND RPGS, ROCKET-PROPELLED GRENADES THAT COULD PUNCTURE ARMOR.

IT WAS SO HARD TO LISTEN, SO HARD TO STAY AWAKE. SO THIRSTY, SO HUNGRY.

AT THE END OF EACH DAY WE SLUMPED DOWN, NO HOPE LEFT IN US.

SNIF!

NORMAN, ARE YOU ALL RIGHT?

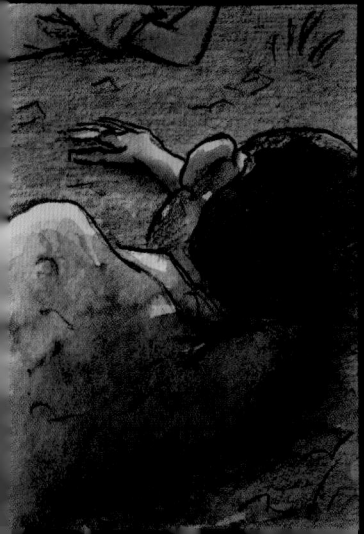

PAUL, TELL US ABOUT AMERICA...

IN AMERICA, MANY PEOPLE WEAR STRANGE THINGS ON THEIR HEADS, HATS OF ALL KINDS, CAPS TOO, SOME ROUND AND OTHERS MADE OF WOOL, NO MATTER WHAT THE TEMPERATURE.

AND THEY HAVE EVERY COLOR OF HAIR, YELLOW AND ORANGE AND BLUE. SOME OF IT STICKS UP IN POINTS. MANY HAVE LONG HAIR THAT CURLS.

BLUE HAIR? *HAHAHA!*

IS EVERYONE RICH IN AMERICA?

I THINK SO. EVERYONE USES ELECTRICITY; EVEN CHILDREN ARE ALLOWED TO TOUCH A SWITCH ON THE WALL.

THE GROUND IS COVERED IN CEMENT AND THERE ARE NO COWS. THERE ARE NO ANIMALS ANYWHERE!

EXCEPT FOR DOGS, AND THEY WALK DOGS ON THE END OF A ROPE...

...AND THE DOGS ARE MADE TO WEAR CLOTHES.

THE GIRL WITH NO EARS...

I HAVE BEEN TO KITGUM. WHAT OF YOUR FAMILY?

A CURSE WAS PUT ON MY FATHER WHEN I WAS VERY YOUNG, AND HE DIED. THEN MY MOTHER DIED TOO, BUT OF TUBERCULOSIS.

I HAD A SISTER, BUT SHE RAN AWAY. THE OTHERS, COUSINS, AUNTS, UNCLES, ARE ALL GONE.

HOW WERE YOU... HOW DID YOU COME TO...?

THE GOVERNMENT REPRESENTATIVES CAME TO OUR VILLAGE AND SAID THAT WE WOULD BE SAFER IN A DISPLACEMENT CAMP. SO MY FRIEND SARAH AND I LEFT OUR VILLAGE AND MOVED INTO THE CAMP.

BUT THE REBELS BROKE INTO THE CAMP AND ABDUCTED MANY CHILDREN. WE WERE AFRAID...

...SO THEN THE GOVERNMENT REPRESENTATIVES SAID THAT IF THE CHILDREN IN THE CAMP WALKED TO GULU, WE WOULD FIND PROTECTION THERE.

YOUR EARS...

WHAT? YOU THINK I SUFFER BECAUSE THEY **TOOK OFF MY EARS?**

THE WOMEN SAY THAT I AM **CURSED**, AND SO THEY LEAVE ME ALONE. THE MEN FIND ME **UGLY**, AND EVEN THE SOLDIERS DO NOT WANT ME TO GO INTO BATTLE BECAUSE THEY SAY THAT I WILL BRING **EVIL SPIRITS** DOWN ON THEM.

BUT I AM LUCKY AND I AM **STRONG**. AS LONG AS I DO NOT GET SICK, I WILL LIVE AND I WILL **ESCAPE**, ONE DAY!

I AM...

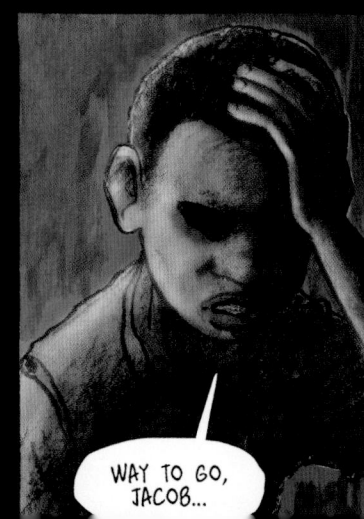

WAY TO GO, JACOB...

THE RAINY SEASON ARRIVED, SLOWLY AT FIRST, DROPLETS IN THE MIDDLE OF THE DAY.

THE DROPS TURNED TO SHOWERS, THE SHOWERS TURNED INTO STORMS.

AND WHEN THE RAIN STOPPED, THE YELLOW SUN SHONE DOWN. THE RAIN SHOULD HAVE COOLED OUR SKIN, BUT IT DID NOT. IT WAS HOT, STICKY WATER THAT EVAPORATED IN AN INSTANT.

MUD CAKED OUR FEET, RAN UP OUR LEGS, AND SPLATTERED INTO OUR FACES AND EYES.

SITTING IN MUD...

SLEEPING IN MUD...

MUD FOR FOOD...

MUD FOR BRAINS.

LIGHTNING THREATENED...

THUNDER CLAPPED...

AND THE RAIN CAME DOWN...

WE WALKED.

DID YOU HEAR? KONY IS NEARBY. THEY SAY THAT HE WILL INSPECT THE TROOPS. WE SHOULD PRAY THAT HE COMES TO BLESS US.

JACOB, DID YOU HEAR THAT?

WHAT DO YOU THINK KONY IS LIKE?

THERE ARE RUMORS HE HAS MAGICAL POWERS, THAT HE HAS THIRTY WIVES AND TWO HUNDRED CHILDREN, AND LIVES LIKE A KING IN SUDAN.

SOME SAY THAT WHEN HE WAS BORN HE STOOD AND WALKED. OTHERS SAY THAT SPIRITS TALK TO HIM AND HE KNOWS THE FUTURE.

THE NEXT DAY CAME AND WENT, AND THE DAY AFTER THAT, AND STILL KONY DID NOT COME.

SPLASH!

WHAT IS IT?
I CAN'T HEAR.

MAYBE THERE
IS AN UNPROTECTED
VILLAGE.

THERE MUST
BE PLENTY OF
FOOD THERE.

FOOD...

FOOD...ONLY SOLDIERS EAT...

...UNLESS WE HAVE FOOD, WE WILL DIE SOON.

NORMAN SURELY WILL, BUT HE IS TOO WEAK TO FIGHT.

IF I JOIN THE BATTLE, I COULD SHARE MY FOOD WITH HIM.

THERE IS A VILLAGE AHEAD. I WILL CHOOSE THE SOLDIERS FOR THE ATTACK.

YOU...YOU...YOU...

I WILL GO!

ME TOO!

YOU CHOOSE *NOW* TO JOIN US?

JACOB, LIZARD DID NOT WANT US, WHY?

I DON'T KNOW...

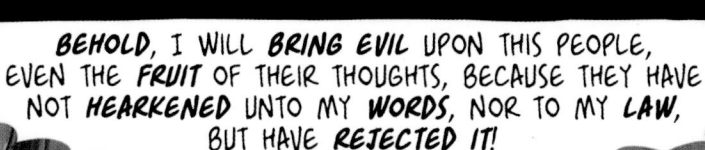

BEHOLD, I WILL **BRING EVIL** UPON THIS PEOPLE, EVEN THE **FRUIT** OF THEIR THOUGHTS, BECAUSE THEY HAVE NOT **HEARKENED** UNTO MY **WORDS**, NOR TO MY **LAW**, BUT HAVE **REJECTED** IT!

GOD IS ON OUR SIDE!

THIS **HOLY WATER** WILL **PROTECT** YOU FROM THE GOVERNMENT **BULLETS**.

MY GRANDMOTHER HAD DIED. TO BE WITHOUT FAMILY IS TO BE ALONE.

MY GRANDMOTHER HAD TAUGHT ME TO COOK. THE GIRLS HERE ARE SO YOUNG. THEY KNOW NOTHING ABOUT FOOD.

WHEN THE COMMANDERS FOUND OUT I COULD COOK, I WAS NOT MADE TO FIGHT.

WHERE ARE WE?

I HEARD THAT WE HAVE CROSSED INTO SUDAN. THE SUDANESE GOVERNMENT SUPPORTS THE LRA.

WAIT!

OTEKA?

IF WE ARE IN SUDAN, WE'RE GOING TO DIE HERE.

I KNOW MY FATHER; WE JUST HAVE TO SURVIVE UNTIL HE SAVES US.

FATHER, PLEASE HURRY...

LISTEN, LISTEN!!

...AND YESTERDAY, THE WORLD COURT IN THE HAGUE CHARGED JOSEPH KONY WITH TWENTY COUNTS OF HUMAN RIGHTS VIOLATIONS AND WILL PROSECUTE HIM WHEN CAPTURED...

WHERE IS THIS WORLD COURT? DOES THIS MEAN PEOPLE KNOW ABOUT US?

ALSO, WE HAVE A MESSAGE FOR THE STUDENTS OF THE GEORGE JONES SEMINARY FOR BOYS... OUR PRAYERS ARE WITH YOU.

HAHA HAHAHA HAHA

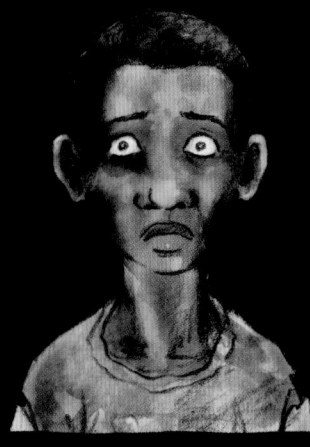

THAT'S IT?

YOU SEE? THEY ARE **NOT COMING** FOR US, WE ARE THE **ENEMY** NOW.

THAT'S NOT TRUE, TONY...

YOU THINK THAT YOU CAN GO HOME? **YOU CANNOT**...

...NONE OF US CAN GO HOME **EVER AGAIN!** WE HAVE SIN IN US NOW, EVIL SPIRITS!

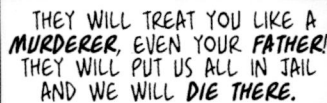

YOU THINK THAT IF YOU DO **NOT KILL** THEY WILL TAKE YOU BACK? THEY WILL **NOT BELIEVE YOU!**

THEY WILL TREAT YOU LIKE A **MURDERER**, EVEN YOUR **FATHER!** THEY WILL PUT US ALL IN JAIL AND WE WILL **DIE THERE**.

THIS IS WHERE WE LIVE NOW. WE ARE **REBEL SOLDIERS**. WE ARE **LRA**. WE ARE KILLING FOR **GOD**, FOR THE **ACHOLI PEOPLE**, FOR **UGANDA**.

TONY, WAIT!

NORMAN, DO NOT BELIEVE HIM, OUR PARENTS ARE COMING FOR US!

DID YOU HEAR THE MESSAGE ON THE RADIO TO YOU AND YOUR CLASSMATES?

YES, OTEKA.

IT WAS CODE. IT SAID, "THE DEAL WILL NOT BE COMPLETED."

WHAT DO YOU MEAN?

THE GOVERNMENT STEPPED IN AND SAID THAT THEY WOULD NOT ALLOW THE EXCHANGE OF GUNS FOR THE STUDENTS. BEWARE OF LIZARD, YOU ARE NO LONGER USEFUL FOR KONY.

BUT...

NO ONE IS COMING FOR US...

IT'S OVER...

JACOB?

JACOB, DO NOT GIVE UP! LISTEN...

DID I TELL YOU THAT IN AMERICA THERE ARE THOUSANDS AND THOUSANDS OF BUILDINGS THAT RISE AS HIGH AS A PLANE FLIES, AND THE BUILDINGS ARE LIT UP WITH LIGHTS, DAY AND NIGHT. THEY KEEP THE ELECTRICITY ON EVEN WHEN NO ONE IS AROUND. CAN YOU BELIEVE THAT?

NO MORE STORIES, PAUL.

NO ONE IS COMING FOR US...

NORMAN, LISTEN TO ME, IT'S GOING TO BE ALL RIGHT...

MY FATHER CAN'T SAVE US...

...THE GOVERNMENT SOLDIERS CAN'T, OR WON'T, SAVE US. WE HAVE NO CHOICE...

...WE HAVE TO SAVE OURSELVES!

YOU MEAN ESCAPE? BUT HOW?

I DON'T KNOW YET...

HANNAH... MAYBE HANNAH CAN HELP.

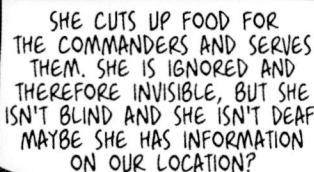

SHE CUTS UP FOOD FOR THE COMMANDERS AND SERVES THEM. SHE IS IGNORED AND THEREFORE INVISIBLE, BUT SHE ISN'T BLIND AND SHE ISN'T DEAF. MAYBE SHE HAS INFORMATION ON OUR LOCATION?

WHY WOULD SHE RISK HER LIFE TO HELP US?

I KNOW SHE IS BRAVE AND SHE TOO WANTS TO ESCAPE.

WE WILL WATCH AND WAIT FOR THE RIGHT TIME.

THERE IS A CONVOY OF GOVERNMENT SOLDIERS COMING OUR WAY. WHO WILL VOLUNTEER TO FIGHT?

YOU! YOU FIGHT TODAY!

ME?

GIVE HIM A PANGA!

SAINT MICHAEL, ARCHANGEL, DEFEND US IN BATTLE. BE OUR DEFENSE AGAINST THE WICKEDNESS AND SNARES OF THE DEVIL. MAY GOD REBUKE HIM, WE HUMBLY PRAY. AND YOU, PRINCE OF THE HEAVENLY HOST, BY THE POWER OF GOD, THRUST INTO HELL SATAN AND THE OTHER EVIL SPIRITS WHO PROWL THE WORLD FOR THE RUIN OF SOULS. AMEN.

GOD IS ON OUR SIDE!

MY FINGERS HURT FROM
HOLDING THE PANGA SO HARD...

...HOW MUCH LONGER ARE
WE GOING TO WAIT?

ATTACK!!

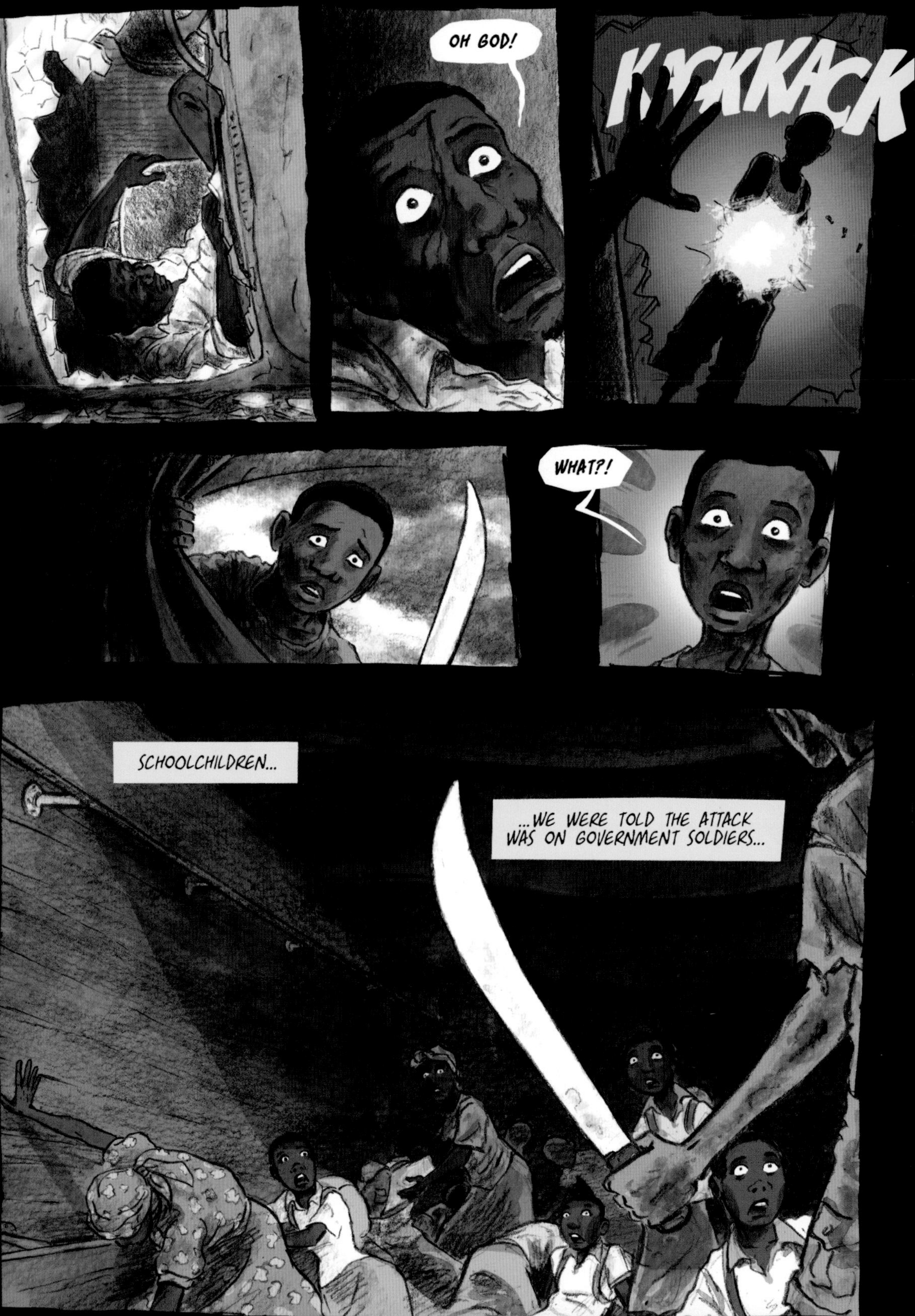

OH GOD!

K-K-KACK

WHAT?!

SCHOOLCHILDREN...

...WE WERE TOLD THE ATTACK WAS ON GOVERNMENT SOLDIERS...

89

KILL THE MOTHER!!

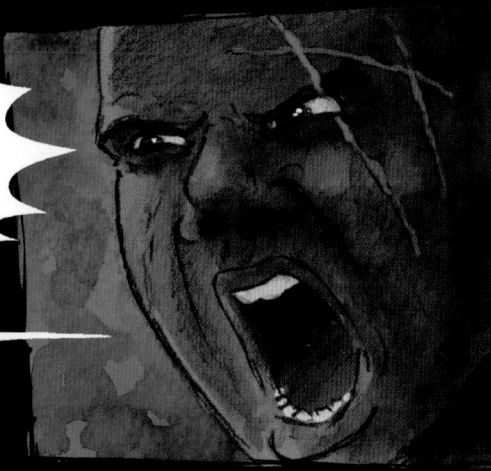

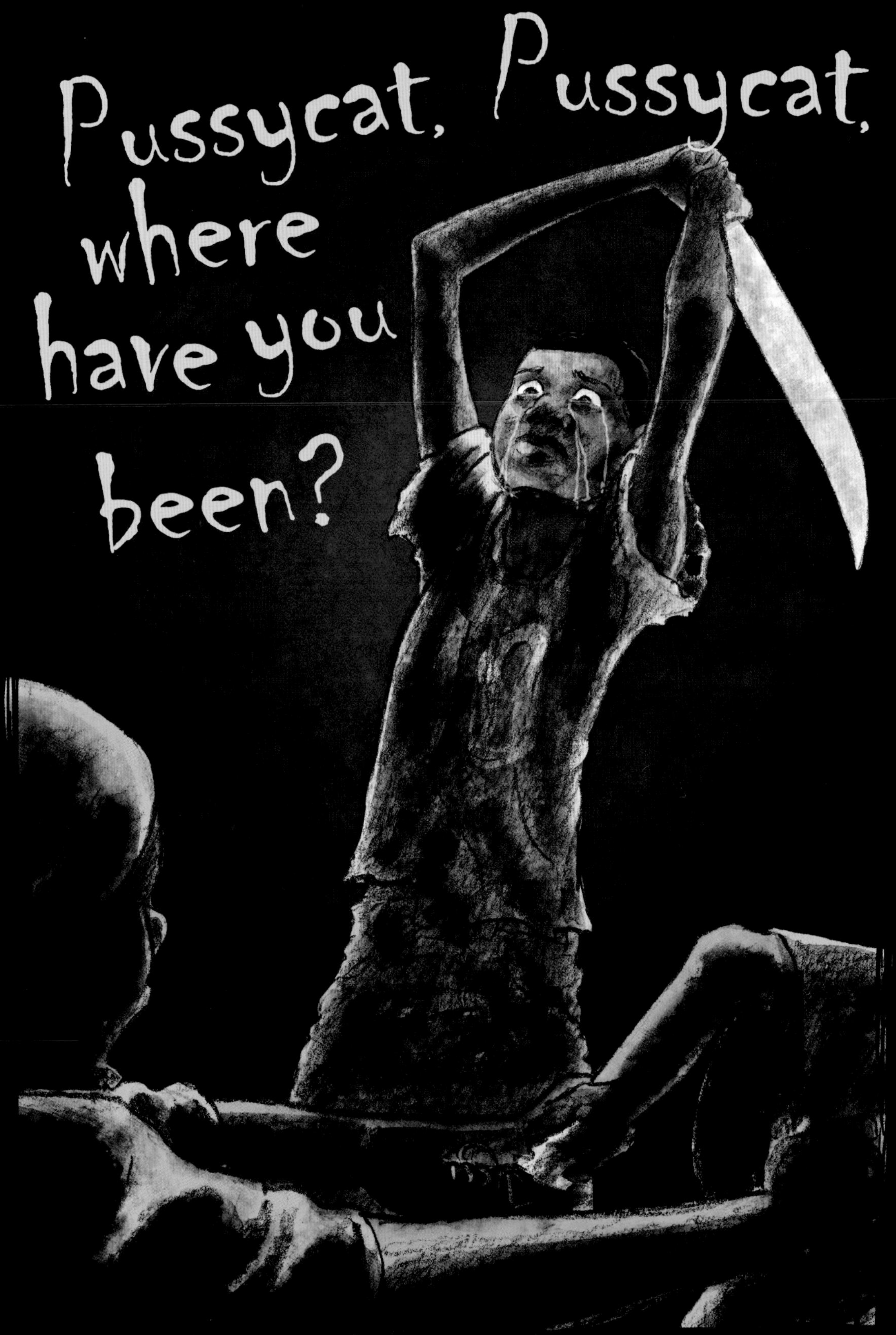
Pussycat, Pussycat,
where
have you
been?

I CANNOT DO THIS...

...I've been to London...

...to visit the Queen...

GET OUT OF THE WAY!

...Pussycat Pussycat...

KACK KA

...what did you do there?

93

95 TIMES 18 EQUALS 1410...

MAYBE...

I DON'T SEE THE NUMBERS ANYMORE.

JACOB, COME EAT!

BUT I DID NOT KILL ANYONE.

WE HAVEN'T KILLED EITHER, BUT WE HAVE TO TRY AND EAT.

MAYBE OTEKA CAN GIVE US FOOD!

KONY HIMSELF HAS DECIDED THAT THOSE STUDENTS WHO HAVE NOT BECOME SOLDIERS WILL BE KILLED. YOU AND YOUR FRIEND MUST ESCAPE TONIGHT!

WE DON'T EVEN KNOW WHERE WE ARE.

WE ARE IN MURCHISON FALLS, THE SAFARI PARK. IF THERE IS ANY TROUBLE, THE TOURISTS WILL STOP COMING AND THE GOVERNMENT WILL LOSE BIG MONEY.

THE GOVERNMENT WILL NOT FIRE ON THE REBELS HERE.

JACOB, MY FATHER BROUGHT ME HERE ONCE. I KNOW WHERE SAMBIYA LODGE IS.

YOU MUST LEAVE NOW. I WILL GUIDE YOU TO THE EDGE OF THE VILLAGE.

LIZARD SUSPECTS YOU. COME WITH US.

MAYBE YOU ARE RIGHT...

ALL RIGHT, FOLLOW ME!

WE CANNOT LEAVE NORMAN BEHIND!

THERE IS NO WAY WE CAN RESCUE HIM.

THERE ARE OVER FOUR HUNDRED SOLDIERS STILL IN CAMP.

YOUR FRIEND IS IN THAT TENT WITH THE GUARD.

HANNAH...

THAT'S HANNAH, SHE WANTS TO ESCAPE TOO!

JACOB, WE CANNOT BRING HER WITH US.

I HAVE TO ASK HER. I WILL GO ALONE.

IF I DO NOT MAKE IT BACK, YOU ESCAPE. TELL MY FATHER THAT I KNOW HE TRIED TO SAVE ME.

TELL EVERYONE ABOUT WHAT HAPPENS HERE.

WE'LL WAIT FOR YOU BY THE SOUTH TRAIL. GOOD LUCK.

WE MUST GET HIM OUT. WE ARE ESCAPING TONIGHT WITH OTEKA. COME WITH US...

THERE ARE TOO MANY COMMANDERS, AND THE GUARD...

I WILL CUT THROUGH THE BACK OF THE TENT.

WHAT ABOUT THE NOISE? THE RIP OF A PANGA SLICING THROUGH CANVAS WILL BE HEARD.

CAN YOU TURN UP THE RADIO?

NOT WITHOUT BEING TOLD TO DO SO.

I'LL FIND A WAY TO TURN UP THE RADIO.

YOU ARE COMING WITH US?

YES!

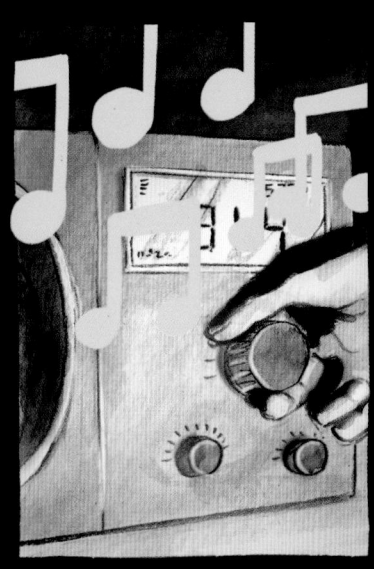

HAS SOMEONE SEEN US LEAVE?

I...I'M NOT SURE...

SAMBIYA LODGE IS ACROSS THE RIVER NILE. HOW ARE WE GOING TO CROSS THE RIVER?

I HEARD THE COMMANDERS SAY THAT NOW THAT THE DEAL WAS OFF TO GET ARMS IN EXCHANGE FOR YOUR LIVES, THEY HAD NO USE FOR THE BOAT. SO MY HOPE IS THAT THERE IS A BOAT ALONG THE RIVER SOMEWHERE THAT WE NEED TO FIND.

THE WHOLE RIVER COMES ALIVE AT NIGHT WITH NILE CROCODILES AND HIPPOPOTAMI WHO FEED AT NIGHT AND JUST BEFORE DAWN.

IF WE DON'T FIND IT, COULD WE JUST SWIM ACROSS?

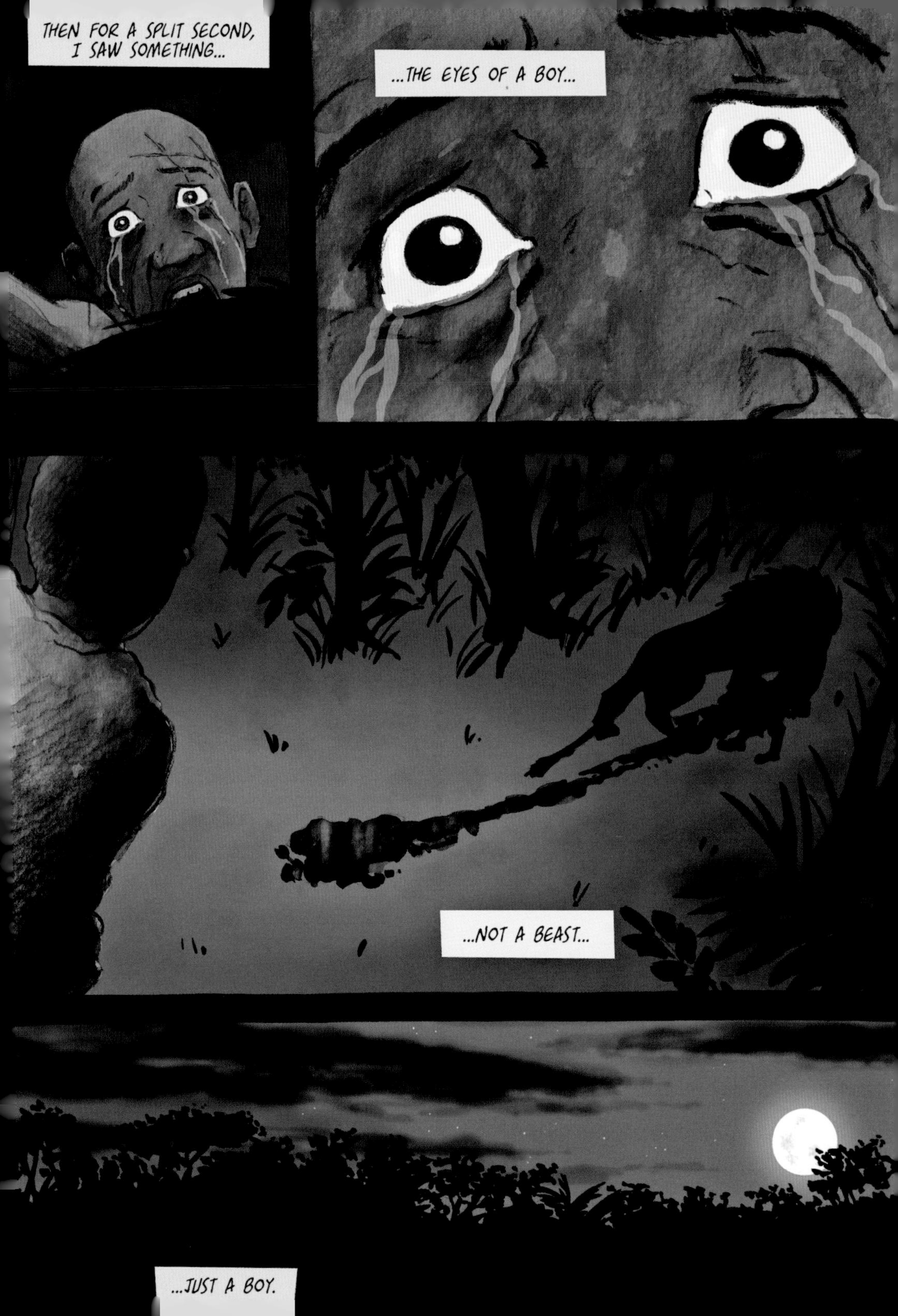

THEN FOR A SPLIT SECOND,
I SAW SOMETHING...

...THE EYES OF A BOY...

...NOT A BEAST...

...JUST A BOY.

WHAT ABOUT THE REBELS?

THEY FLED WHEN THE LION ATTACKED.

WE MUST GO NOW BEFORE THEY COME BACK.

SNIF!

WAIT, SOMEONE'S THERE...

SNIF!

TONY, IS THAT YOU?

I'M SORRY, JACOB.

COME WITH US, BROTHER.

NOW WE HAVE TO FIND THE BOAT.

WE HAVE TO SPLIT UP AND STAY HIDDEN. I WILL GO WEST ALONG THE RIVER. NORMAN AND PAUL, YOU GO EAST. COUNT OUT ONE THOUSAND STEPS AND THEN TURN BACK.

WE WILL CLIMB BACK UP THE BANK AND WALK ALONG THE RIDGE.

LOOK FOR A FRESHLY MADE PATH BACK DOWN TO THE RIVER. WHOEVER LEFT THE BOAT WOULD HAVE MARKED THE PLACE IN SOME WAY.

YOU ARE RIGHT TO WORRY ABOUT HIM.

THE COMMANDERS CAN TELL WHICH BOYS CAN BE BROKEN LIKE GLASS. SHATTERED GLASS CANNOT BE PUT BACK TOGETHER. WHEN THE GOOD BOYS BECOME LRA, THEY BECOME ESPECIALLY MEAN, ESPECIALLY DANGEROUS. I HAVE SEEN IT HAPPEN OVER AND OVER.

HAVE YOU EVER...

...I'M SORRY...

HAVE I EVER KILLED?

NO. I WAS CONSIDERED TOO USELESS TO BE A SOLDIER. I WAS A SLAVE AND A SERVANT, BUT BECAUSE I SERVED FOOD I WAS ABLE TO STEAL AND EAT. AND I WAS NEVER CAUGHT.

IF WE LIVE, WHAT WILL YOU DO?

I WILL JOIN THE NUNS AND BECOME A TEACHER. IT IS WHAT I PLANNED.

I KNOW THE NAMES OF MANY CHILDREN WHO WERE CAPTURED AND KILLED. I REPEAT THEIR NAMES TO MYSELF BEFORE I SLEEP.

ONE DAY, I WILL TELL PARENTS WHAT HAPPENED TO THEIR CHILDREN. ONE DAY, I WILL TELL THE WHOLE WORLD. IF PEOPLE KNOW WHAT HAPPENS TO CHILDREN LIKE US, THEY WILL HELP.

THERE IS A MAN WHO COMES OFTEN TO MY FATHER'S HOUSE. HIS NAME IS MUSA HENRY TORAC. HIS GRANDSON WAS ABDUCTED, I DO NOT KNOW WHEN.

HIS NAME IS MICHAEL.

HAVE YOU HEARD OF HIM?

WHAT?

DO YOU KNOW HIM?

YOU KNOW HIM TOO.

YOU KNOW HIM BY THE NAME OF LIZARD.

124

WE HAVE FOUND THE BOAT!

IT'S NOT FAR AND THERE ARE NO GUARDS!

HOW BIG IS IT?

BIG ENOUGH. WE MUST GO NOW!

THE BOAT WAS EASY TO FIND. THEY CUT A MANGO TREE TO MARK THE PATH DOWN TO THE RIVER.

LOOK!

AMAZING...

HURRY!

PERHAPS THE REBELS THOUGHT GOVERNMENT SOLDIERS MIGHT BE TOO CLOSE.

PERHAPS KONY WAS HOLDING TO THE AGREEMENT NOT TO ATTACK ON PARK LAND AND FRIGHTEN THE WEALTHY TOURISTS.

THE REBELS WOULD BE ON THE MARCH, AND WITH THEM THE REST OF THE BOYS FROM THE GEORGE JONES SEMINARY FOR BOYS, LIKELY LOST FOREVER.

I TRY NOT TO THINK OF THEM. I TRY REALLY, REALLY HARD.

WE TRIED TO PADDLE, BUT WE WERE SO TIRED.

THE CURRENT CARRIED US ALONG.

WHAT?

LOOK!

LOOK AT THE SIGN.

SAMBIYA LODGE 2 KM →

WE'VE MADE IT!

SPLASH!

WAIT! WE MUST GO UNARMED, OTHERWISE GOVERNMENT SOLDIERS WILL SHOOT AT FIRST SIGHT.

I AM THE SMALLEST, SO I'LL WALK IN FRONT. THEY MIGHT NOT KILL ME.

2 KM →

FATHER, I'M ALMOST HOME...

STOP!!

DON'T SHOOT!

WE HAVE ESCAPED THE REBELS. WE WANT TO COME HOME.

YOU TOOK MY SISTER! SHE WAS WALKING TO SCHOOL!

PLEASE, WE ARE TIRED AND WE NEED FOOD...

WHERE IS MY SISTER?

THUK!

I DON'T KNOW... PLEASE, WE ARE STUDENTS OF THE GEORGE JONES SEMINARY FOR BOYS.

MY NAME IS KITINO JACOB.

WHAT DID YOU SAY YOUR NAME IS?

GULU...

FATHER, I AM HOME!

BODA-BODA BOYS ZOOMED ABOUT ON THEIR MOTORCYCLES, WOMEN WENT TO MARKET WITH BABIES ON THEIR BACKS...

...BICYCLES AND SMILES EVERYWHERE.

MY HEART BEGAN TO BEAT FASTER AND FASTER...

GET OUT!

VVRRRRMMM

JACOB!!

WAIT!!

HANNAH...

AND JUST LIKE THAT, HANNAH WAS GONE.

THE COUNSELORS SAID THAT IT WAS BEST IF WE STAYED IN THE REHABILITATION CENTER FOR A FEW WEEKS.

FATHER ARGUED. HE WANTED ME HOME RIGHT AWAY. BUT IN THE END, FATHER RELENTED.

THE POLICE INTERROGATED US. THEY DID NOT SEEM TO CARE ABOUT HOW WE WERE TREATED BY THE LRA. THEY ONLY WANTED TO KNOW ABOUT THE GUNS AND FUTURE PLANS OF KONY AND HIS CREW. HOW WOULD WE KNOW SUCH THINGS?

THERE WERE DOCTORS, NURSES, AND SOCIAL WORKERS TO TEND TO US, PEOPLE WHO SAID THAT WE MUST BE REINTEGRATED INTO SOCIETY. THEY SAID THAT WE MUST FORGIVE OURSELVES...

...FORGIVE OURSELVES?

WE HAD BEEN STOLEN...

IMPRISONED...

TORTURED...

ABUSED...

WHOM SHOULD WE FORGIVE?

I SAID NOTHING.

WE ATE IN SILENCE.

NORMAN SLEPT A GREAT DEAL.

I WOULD WAKE WITH A START AT THE SLIGHTEST SOUND...

...MY HEART RACING.

SNIF...

TONY?

MY MOTHER IS COMING AGAIN TODAY...

THAT IS GOOD.

THE NEIGHBORS CALL HER THINGS, BAD WORDS, EVIL WORDS, BECAUSE OF ME.

THEY KNOW THAT I AM A RETURNEE.

MY LITTLE BROTHER THINKS I'M A KILLER. HE IS AFRAID OF ME.

WOULD TONY HAVE KILLED US, I WONDER SOMETIMES, IF HE'D BEEN ORDERED TO?

THE NEXT DAY I LEARNED THAT OTEKA LEFT DURING THE NIGHT.

WHY DIDN'T HE SAY GOODBYE?

NORMAN, ARE YOU OKAY?

MY FATHER CAME THIS MORNING.

HE SAID THAT HE LOVED ME, BUT HE WOULD NOT TAKE ME BACK YET. HE IS AFRAID OF ME, I CAN FEEL IT.

RETURNING HOME WASN'T HOW I THOUGHT IT WOULD BE.

TWICE WE HAD TO GO TO THE HOSPITAL FOR SOME TESTS.

THE RECEPTIONIST HAD HEARD ABOUT US RETURNEES.

THE NURSE WILL CALL YOU WHEN THE DOCTOR IS READY TO SEE YOU.

THERE WAS A LARGE COURTYARD WHERE PEOPLE WAITED TO SEE THE DOCTORS.

THE WAIT WAS LONG...

IT WAS HOT EVEN IN THE SHADE...

PEOPLE WATCHED US...

THEY THOUGHT WE WERE KILLERS WITH A THIRST TO KILL AGAIN...

ONE DAY, MUSA HENRY TORAC CAME TO SEE ME.

I PRAYED FOR YOUR SAFE RETURN EVERY DAY, AND NOW MY PRAYERS ARE ANSWERED.

I KNOW WHAT HAPPENED TO MICHAEL...

YOU KNOW WHERE MY GRANDSON IS?

HE IS WITH GOD.

ARE YOU SURE? YOU HAVE NEVER MET HIM, HE...

I AM SURE. HE WAS...

YOUR GRANDSON WAS A GOOD BOY. HE WAS KILLED BECAUSE HE WAS A GOOD BOY. HE DID NOT SUFFER

YES, HE WAS A GOOD BOY.

I LOVED HIM VERY MUCH. I LOVE HIM STILL.

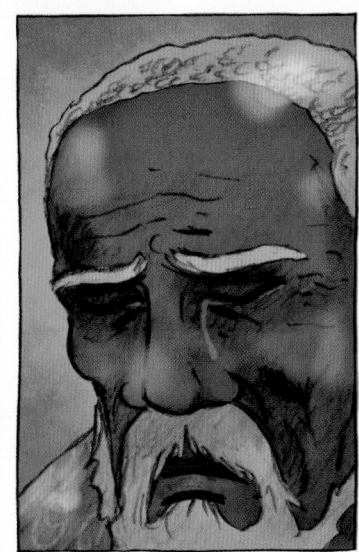

THANK YOU, JACOB. IT MUST HAVE BEEN HARD TO TELL AN OLD MAN THAT HIS GRANDSON IS DEAD. THE TRUTH IS IMPORTANT.

WHAT IS A LIE? KONY AND HIS COMMANDERS LIED TO US OVER AND OVER AGAIN AND CAUSED GREAT PAIN.

NOW I HAVE LIED. WILL MY LIE CAUSE PAIN OR ALLOW A GRANDFATHER TO HEAL?

JACOB, A LETTER HAS ARRIVED. GOOD NEWS!

TONY AND NORMAN GOT LETTERS TOO! WE HAVE BEEN ACCEPTED INTO A SCHOOL IN KAMPALA. NO ONE WILL KNOW US THERE. WE CAN START AGAIN.

WE LEAVE TOMORROW!

TOMORROW?

DO NOT WORRY. WE WILL BE FRIENDS FOREVER.

I WILL COME TO KAMPALA WITH MY FATHER AS OFTEN AS I CAN.

THE NEXT MORNING EVERYTHING HAPPENED QUICKLY.

JACOB, WHAT WILL YOU DO?

150

I WILL GO BACK TO SCHOOL. AND MAYBE ONE DAY I WILL BE ABLE TO TELL PEOPLE ABOUT US. MAYBE IF THEY KNEW, THEY WOULD HELP. IT IS WHAT HANNAH BELIEVES.

I HOPE TONY WILL FIND A WAY TO FORGIVE HIMSELF.

I WILL TAKE CARE OF NORMAN AND TONY LIKE YOU TOOK CARE OF US.

I KNOW THAT YOU WILL, PAUL.

BROTHERS.

BROTHERS.

BROTHERS.

VVVVRRRRR

JACOB, YOUR FATHER IS SENDING A CAR FOR YOU SHORTLY.

THANK YOU.

THERE WILL BE OTHER RETURNEES LIKE YOU. MORE CHILD SOLDIERS WILL FIND A WAY OUT OF THE BUSH.

YOU CAN HELP THEM. YOU CAN COME BACK HERE AND TALK TO THEM.

YES, PERHAPS I WILL.

COME JACOB, LET US GO HOME.

ETHEL, I WOULD LIKE TO WALK HOME.

BUT...

YOU DON'T THINK I CAN FIND MY WAY ACROSS THE CITY I WAS BORN IN?

YOU HAVE GROWN. I WILL HAVE TO GET USED TO THIS NEW JACOB.

I SHALL HAVE DINNER WAITING FOR YOU WHEN YOU ARRIVE HOME.

EVERYTHING LOOKS THE SAME, BUT SOMEHOW DIFFERENT.

I SEE THE COLORS, SEE THE BEAUTY, BUT I DON'T FEEL SAFE ANYMORE.

I FEEL LIKE AT ANY MOMENT THE LRA COULD FLOOD INTO THE CITY LIKE A TORRENT OF RAIN AND TAKE ME AWAY AGAIN.

DON'T THEY KNOW THAT ONE DAY THEIR BABIES COULD BE TAKEN AWAY AND MADE TO KILL?

WHY DO SUCH THINGS HAPPEN?

HELLO, JACOB!

OTEKA! HOW DID YOU KNOW I WAS HERE?

I WAS WATCHING THE CENTER ALL MORNING. I SAW THE BUS TAKE THE BOYS AWAY AND FOLLOWED YOU HERE.

THEY ARE GOING TO SCHOOL IN KAMPALA. IT IS GOOD. BUT WHERE DID YOU GO?

A WOMAN TOOK CARE OF ME FOR MANY YEARS. I WENT BACK TO HER GRAVE TO SAY A PROPER GOODBYE.

I AM GLAD TO SEE YOU. IT IS HARD TO TALK ABOUT THINGS TO PEOPLE WHO CANNOT UNDERSTAND.

I TOO AM TROUBLED. BUT TELL ME, WHAT ARE YOU THINKING?

I WAS THINKING ABOUT TONY AND LIZARD AND WONDERING ABOUT ME.

YOU WERE WONDERING IF YOU COULD HAVE KILLED?

YES.

DO YOU THINK OF THE LION?

ALWAYS.

THE LION IS A MIGHTY BEAST. HE HUNTS WITH NOBILITY. BUT WHEN HE IS OLD AND CAST OUT OF HIS PRIDE, HE TOO WILL KILL TO SURVIVE. WE ARE NO DIFFERENT.

ARE WE ALL BEASTS? IS THIS OUR NATURE?

NO, JACOB, WE CAN CHOOSE. THAT IS GOD'S GIFT.

I CHOOSE TO RETURN TO THE BUSH AND HELP GOVERNMENT SOLDIERS RESCUE ABDUCTED CHILDREN.

NO, OTEKA. YOU WILL BE RECOGNIZED!

THIS IS MY DESTINY. I FEEL IT.

THEN I WILL COME WITH YOU.

NO. I HEARD YOU TELL PAUL THAT YOU WANT PEOPLE TO KNOW ABOUT US. SO TELL THE WORLD, JACOB. TELL THEM THAT WE ARE THE SAME...

...JUST CHILDREN TRYING TO SURVIVE.

BROTHER

BROTHER, I WILL SEE YOU AGAIN.

WELCOME HOME, MY SON.

THIS NEW FOOTBALL'S BEEN WAITING FOR YOU FOR MUCH TOO LONG.

THANK YOU, FATHER!

YOU WILL SEE, EVERYTHING WILL BE ALL RIGHT NOW.

AT FIRST
I TRIED
TO FORGET.

EVERYONE WORRIED
ABOUT ME, ESPECIALLY
FATHER.

OVER AND OVER
I ASKED MYSELF,
"WHAT SHOULD
I DO?"

WHAT IS
MY PURPOSE?

DAYS...

NIGHTS...

WEEKS PASSED.

The lion roared.
He leapt. We hear Li
Then I saw something
The eyes of a boy
not a beast—
just a boy

MONTHS PASSED.

AND THEN IT GOT A LITTLE EASIER.

JACOB, YOU HAVE A VISITOR.

161

HELLO, JACOB!

HANNAH!?

HANNAH!!
I'M SO GLAD
TO SEE YOU AGAIN!

HAHA,
GLAD TO SEE
YOU TOO, JACOB!

OH SORRY,
I DIDN'T...

WHAT'S
WRONG?

I MEAN,
ARE YOU A
NUN NOW?

NO, I AM LIVING WITH THE NUNS AND I AM STUDYING TO BE A TEACHER.

WILL YOU... I MEAN, MIGHT YOU EVER BECOME A NUN?

I DO NOT THINK IT WOULD BE RIGHT FOR ME. I STAY WITH THE NUNS BECAUSE I HAVE NO FAMILY.

YOU HAVE FAMILY.

COME AND MEET MY FATHER.

DEAR READER

AS BEST AS I CAN TELL IT, THIS IS OUR STORY. MANY YEARS HAVE PASSED AND I
WOULD LIKE TO REPORT THAT KONY AND HIS LORD'S RESISTANCE ARMY NO LONGER
EXIST – BUT THAT WOULD NOT BE TRUE. WHILE KONY HAS LOST MUCH OF HIS POWER,
HE CONTINUES TO CARRY ON HIS CRIMES ACROSS THE BORDER IN THE CONGO OR DRC.

TO THINK BACK TO THOSE TIMES CAUSES ME GREAT ANGUISH, BUT IT HAS BROUGHT
INSIGHT TOO. HINDSIGHT ALLOWS ME TO SEE MICHAEL, THE BOY WHO CALLED HIMSELF
LIZARD, AS BOTH A VICTIM AND AN ENEMY.

AFTER MANY DANGEROUS TREKS IN THE BUSH, OTEKA ARRIVES AT MY HOUSE IN GULU.
HANNAH PREPARES HIS FAVORITE FOOD, THEN WE SIT OUT UNDER THE STARS AND ASK
OURSELVES: WHERE DOES THE VICTIM END AND THE CRIMINAL BEGIN? WHOM DO WE
PUNISH? WHO IS ACCOUNTABLE? WHAT HAPPENS WHEN THE CHILD BECOMES AN ADULT
AND CONTINUES HIS OR HER PATH OF DESTRUCTION? THIS WORLD WILL SEE MANY MORE
CHILDREN LIKE MICHAEL. THESE ARE QUESTIONS THAT MUST BE ANSWERED.

I RECALL TOO HOW KONY AND HIS COMMANDERS TWISTED THE WORDS OF GOD. MY
FAITH WAVERED WHEN I WAS A CAPTIVE, BUT IT HAS RETURNED TO ME JUST AS I HAVE
RETURNED TO MY FAMILY.

THIS IS THE END OF OUR STORY. HANNAH BELIEVES THAT IF THE WORLD KNOWS THAT
CHILD SOLDIERS SUFFER UNIMAGINABLE CRUELTY AND PAIN, THEN HELP WILL COME.

I HOPE THIS IS RIGHT.

JACOB
GULU, UGANDA, 2012.

THE END

POSTSCRIPT

This is a book of fiction based on interviews in Gulu, Uganda. Everything that happened in this book has happened, and is happening still. The Lord's Resistance Army continues to torment, abduct, and murder children. There are as many 250,000 child soldiers in over 35 countries. We can realize a world without child soldiers.

ACKNOWLEDGMENTS

The research for *War Brothers*, the novel, was done in Gulu, Uganda. Great thanks, then and now, to Julia Bell, traveler; Adrian Bradbury, founder of Gulu Walk; Akullo Evelyn Otwili, translator; Okello Moses Rubangangeyo, former captive and lieutenant of the LRA. Other names have been held back at their request. In Canada, Thomas Edward Otto, LL.B., and Opiyo Oloya, school principal.

The original editor and copy editor of *War Brothers*, the novel—Barbara Berson and Catherine Marjoribanks—were always a phone call away.

The Annick team includes: Alison Kooistra, consulting editor; Chandra Wohleber, managing editor; Kong Njo, designer; and Katie Hearn, who wrapped it up.

Finally J. Torris for being the Great Connector, and Tim Wynne-Jones, 'nuff said.

ABOUT THE AUTHORS

Sharon E. McKay is a multi-award-winning writer and Canadian War Artist (CFAP-vet). She is the author of *Charlie Wilcox* (set in France and Newfoundland), *Thunder over Kandahar* (set in Afghanistan), and *Enemy Territory* (set in Israel and the West Bank). A fearless world traveler, Sharon developed the story line for *War Brothers* in northern Uganda. She divides her time between Charlottetown, Prince Edward Island, and Toronto, Canada. Visit her website at www.sharonmckay.com.

Daniel Lafrance is a professional storyboard artist and has had many short comics published. *War Brothers* is his first graphic novel. Originally from Quebec, he now lives in Toronto with his wonderful wife Nadia and his amazing son Maxime. Visit his website at www.danlafrance.com.